Lauren Child

Slightly INVISIBLE

Featuring

Charlie and Lola

with a special
appearance by
Soren
Lorensen

CANDLEWICK PRESS

For the original Marv
and his sister, Martha, and
his brother, Vincent,

and

for Conrad and his brother, Enzo

First U.S. paperback edition 2016

First published in Great Britain in 2010 by Orchard Books, London

Library of Congress Catalog Card Number 2010038710
ISBN 978-0-7636-5347-7 (hardcover) / ISBN 978-0-7636-9014-4 (paperback)

16 17 18 19 20 21 WKT 10 9 8 7 6 5 4 3 2 1

Printed in Shenzhen, Guangdong, China

This book was typeset in
Officina Serif Book and Badloc.
The illustrations were done in mixed media.

Candlewick Press
99 Dover Street
Somerville, Massachusetts 02144

visit us at www.candlewick.com

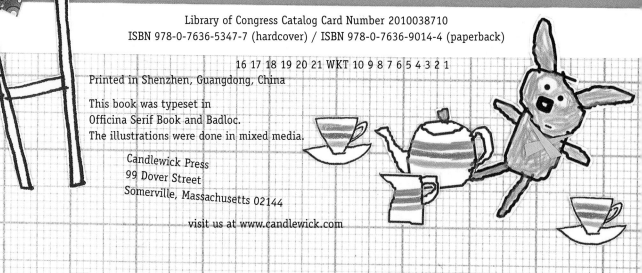

I have this little sister, Lola.
She is small and very funny.
She always wants to know what I am up to, and
she always wants to do what I am doing.
She NEVER wants to be anywhere without me.

Most of the time this is fine.
But sometimes I just want to be by myself
ON MY OWN with just Marv.

Marv is my best friend, and usually we like
to spend our time looking for strange
and tricky creatures.

Lola does
not think
this is fun.

Last week Mary and I were busy floating in OUTER SPACE looking for

martians,

and Lola stepped on our spaceship.

We had to **walk** back to Earth.

And one time,

when we had just discovered this amazing

SEA MONSTER at the bottom of the ocean,

Lola said she wanted to take it for a ride in her cart.

And yesterday,

just when

Marv and I

were

creeping up on the most STRANGE and

terrifyingly **tricky** creature in the UNIVERSE,

Lola's rabbit made a **squeaking** noise and he ran off.

So this time I said,

"Today, Lola, just for once, I want to play with Marv by **myself** on my own.

You see, we are inventing a very **inventive** invention."

"What **IS** it?" says Lola.

"It's **top secret**," I say.

"What's it **top secret** for?" says Lola.

"It's a potion for helping us catch **strange** and **tricky** creatures," says Marv.

"Oh," says Lola. "How does it **do that?**"

"By turning you **invisible,**" Marv says.

"Oh," says Lola. "Would you maybe like to have a **tea party** instead?"

"LOLA!" I say,
"Will you STOP bothering us
and interrupting!"

Lola says,

"I will NOT

do

bothering, and I will
NOT do interrupting.
You
won't even
know
I am here."

So Marv and I invent an **INVISIBILITY** potion.

It is made from pink milk, a tiny drop of banana,

and a **SECRET INVISIBLE INGREDIENT** that no one except us can see.

We leave it in the fridge, and when we have sailed twice around the world and seen some **EXTREMELY** strange creatures, but not **ONE** single tricky one,

we decide to

have a snack.

Sailing around the world can make you quite peckish.

But when we go into the kitchen,
we get a bit of a fright because there

is a STRANGE and

terrifyingly **tricky** creature,

looking very hungry indeed.

There is
no escape.

"Lola!" I shout. "What have you done with our potion?"
But Lola is nowhere to be seen.
We look **everywhere**.

But all we can hear is a tiny voice. . . .

"where are you?"

It sounds as if it is coming from a long way away.

I shout.

"I am over here. You **probably** cannot see me because I am *invisible.*"

But when I look under Mom and Dad's bed, there she is, talking away.

"Who are you talking to?" I say.

"My friend Soren Lorensen,"
says Lola.

I say, "LOLA, did you drink our
invisibility potion?"

Lola says,
"Oh, I only had a small sip.
Soren Lorensen had much more than
I did. That's why he is more
invisible than me."

I say, "You are NOT INVISIBLE,
not even one bit."

"How do you know?" says Lola.

"Because we can SEE you,
of course," says Marv.

And Lola says,
"You can only see me because
you know what I look like.
You can't see Soren Lorensen
at all."

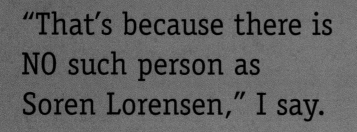

"That's because there is NO such person as Soren Lorensen," I say.

"Well, if there is no such **person**,"

"Lola," I say, "now we will never catch the MOST STRANGE and terrifyingly **tricky** creature in the universe."

"Why not?"
says Lola.

"Because we can't CREEP UP on him," says Marv.

"Don't worry,"
says Lola.
"Soren Lorensen will **catch** him."

"Really?"
I say.

"Oh, yes," says Lola.
"All you will need is
a tea set
and a little cart
and also a rabbit, of course."

"REALLY?" I say.

"Oh yes,
and you MUST
absolutely get one or
three glasses of
pink milk, too."

"WHAT?
All the
pink milk?"
says Marv.

"Yes,
completely,"
says Lola.

So we set off to find the MOST STRANGE and terrifyingly tricky creature in the universe.

I say, "What is the tea set for, Lola?"

And she says, "Tricky creatures love tea."

And Marv says,

"What is the rabbit for, Lola?"

"But why do we need a little cart?" I say.

Lola says, "For the pink milk, of course."

And Mary says, "What is the pink milk for, Lola?"

frightened of rabbits."

are creatures

Tricky

you up.

gobbling

creature from the stop

"To

And Lola says,

And Lola

says,

"You will see."

Soon we find ourselves right in the middle of the deep, dark forest where the MOST STRANGE and terrifyingly tricky creature lives.

And Lola whispers, "Shhh, Soren Lorensen is talking, and he says we must be very, extremely quiet.

Don't make even a squeak."

"I can't hear him talking," says Marv.

"You can't **hear** him because he is INVISIBLE," says Lola.

"You CAN hear invisible people," I say.

Lola says, "Not Soren Lorensen, because his **voice** is invisible **too**."

Marv says, "There are no such things as **invisible** voices."

Lola says,
"If there are no such things as invisible voices, then why can't you hear him?"

"SHHH," I whisper. "Something is coming."

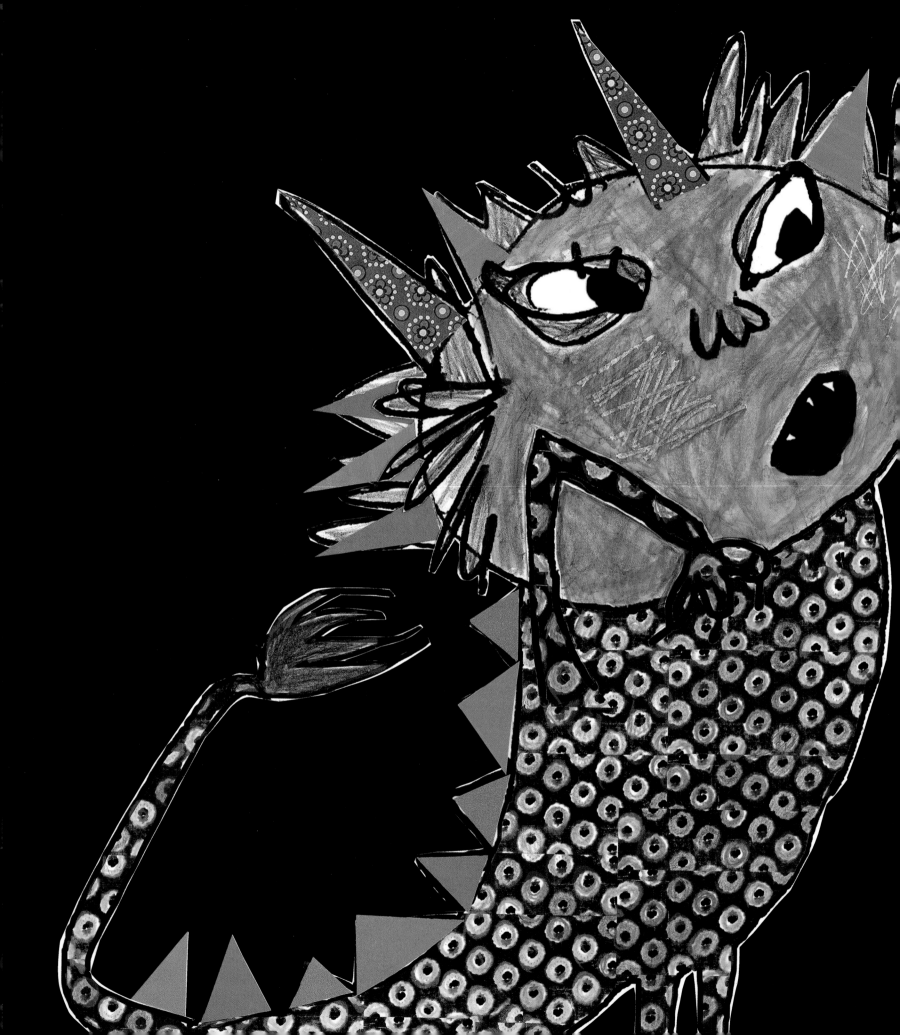

AND THEN THERE HE IS,

the most **strange** and terrifyingly **tricky** creature in the universe, about to gobble us up . . .

"Show him the rabbit!"

says Lola.

And just like that

we have

CAUGHT

HIM.

And there is
no escape for
the MOST STRANGE
and
terrifyingly tricky creature
in the
universe.

"See?" shouts Lola.
"I **told** you Soren Lorensen knew how to
         catch the most **strangest** and
                            TRICKY creature."

"How did he do it?" I say.

"Well," says Lola,
         "EVERYBODY loves tea parties."

"So who gets to drink the
pink milk?" says Marv.

"Oh, that is for
       Soren Lorensen,"
              says Lola.

"Catching strange
and tricky creatures
makes him quite
     thirsty."

"Now,"
says Lola,

"it was fun
to play with
you and Marv,
but please
DON'T do any
bothering or
interrupting...."

"Soren Lorensen would like to
drink his pink milk all by himself,
with just me on his own."